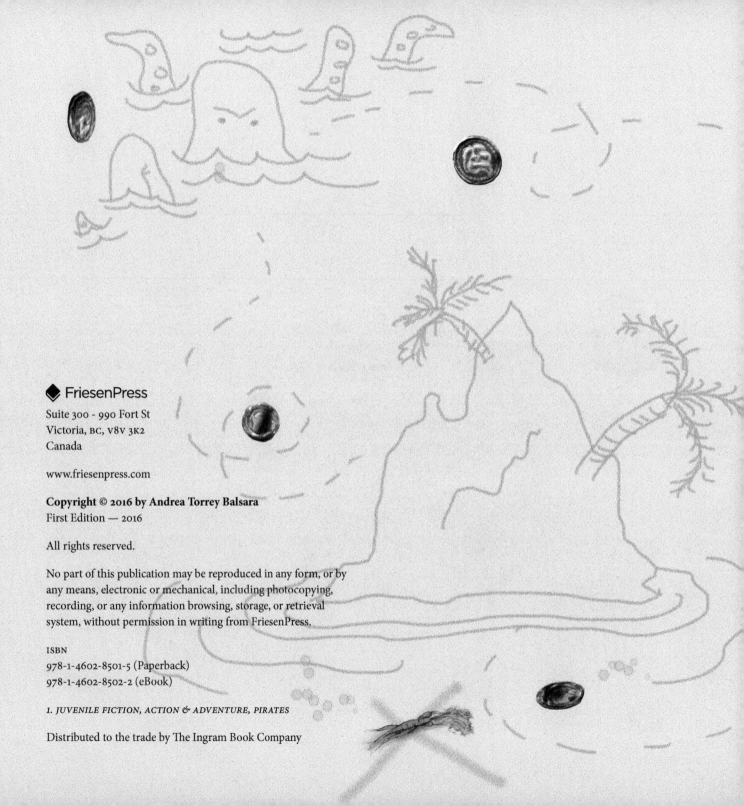

◆ FriesenPress

Suite 300 - 990 Fort St
Victoria, BC, V8V 3K2
Canada

www.friesenpress.com

ISBN
978-1-4602-8501-5 (Paperback)
978-1-4602-8502-2 (eBook)

1. JUVENILE FICTION, ACTION & ADVENTURE, PIRATES

Distributed to the trade by The Ingram Book Company

To my family

You've helped me sail through rough waters,
man the bilge pumps, and navigate by the stars.
I love you all!

ATB

GREENBEARD
the Pirate Pig

Story & art by

Andrea Torrey Balsara

In a garden on top of a tall hill that overlooked the sea, a simple farmer tended his lettuce and carrots.

That farmer's name was GREENBEARD.

His name was Greenbeard because he loved lettuce, which he ate until his beard turned green.

But he loved his carrots, too.

He was, after all, a guinea pig.

Greenbeard lived a simple life, and he was happy,
until one day a fine salt breeze…

blew in from the sea… up the hill…

and through his garden.
He took a deep,

deep

breath.

Like you and me, he'd heard tales of pirates who sailed the seven seas. As Greenbeard sniffed the sea air, he imagined the roll of a ship under his paws... the whistle of wind in his whiskers... the roughness of grit in his claws.

"Greenbeard, my fine pig," he said to himself, "that's the smell of... adventure!"

Greenbeard packed his bag.

He pulled his carrots,
and he bundled
his lettuce.

He brushed his boots
(used only for special occasions)
to a shine.

He shook the dust from his garden hat and
looked at himself in the mirror.

Turning from side to side, he said, "Hmmm.
It needs a little… something."

Greenbeard strapped his garden belt across his chest so it looked more piratey.

Next, he folded up the sides of his hat, plucked a crisp leaf of lettuce, and stuck it in the rim.

The lettuce leaf fluttered jauntily in the breeze, and to Greenbeard, it looked just like the feather in a pirate's hat.

"Perfect!" he said.

Greenbeard pulled one last carrot from the earth, shook off the dirt, and put it in his belt. "After all," he said, "every pirate needs a sword."

And then the simple farmer left his garden...

and walked down the hill....

Mmm...mmm...

to the sea below.

And as he walked, he hummed and sang,

"Mmm...mmm...a pirate pig I be...

Mmm...mmm...I sail the seven seas...

Mmm...wind in my whiskers...mmm...

Grit in my claws...mmm...mmm..."

Mmm...mmm...

Mmm

 When he reached the water, Greenbeard saw
a small ship leaning on its side against a dock.

An old mouse looked at Greenbeard, then at the ship, then
back at Greenbeard. "It's a very good ship!" he squeaked
nervously. "Yes, yes! A very, *very* . . . good ship!"

Greenbeard peered at the ship.
"Do you think it will float?" he asked the mouse.

"Yes, yes, of course it will!
Or I *think* it will."

The old mouse wiped his glasses.
"But the price is cheap.
It's yours for a song!"

"Mine for a song?"
asked Greenbeard.
"Then I shall sing one for
you now!"

He took a deep breath and
opened his mouth wide
to sing.

"No, no, no," said the mouse.
"Not for a *real* song.
I mean that because the ship needs
(*cough*)... a little work,
it can be yours...

cheap!"

"Arrrr! But not cheap enough!"
growled a gloomy voice.
A rat stepped from the shadows.

"That tub will take you straight to

DAVY JONES'S LOCKER!"

"Oh, that's just Snug Rumkin,"
squeaked the old mouse. "Don't listen to *him!*"
But Greenbeard stepped forward.
"Mr. Rumkin. Could you tell me, where is this
Mr. Davy Jones's Locker?"

The rat squinted at him.
"Why, it's at the bottom of the sea!
Where monsters dwell and dead pirates sail!"

"Ah, what adventure!"

said Greenbeard. "I'll take it!"

Snug Rumkin
groaned and shook
his head.

Greenbeard worked hard on his ship.

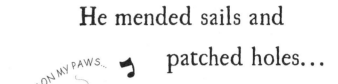

...WIND IN MY WHISKERS...

He mended sails and
patched holes...

...SALT ON MY PAWS...

He whittled,
and he sewed...

...MOLD ON MY BISCUITS...GRIT IN MY CLAWS...

And on the back, he painted the ship's name...

THE GOLDEN LETTUCE

And then he scrubbed,
and he polished, and he tidied until...
The Golden Lettuce gleamed!

But as Greenbeard began to climb down, a rope tangled around his boot, and... he plunged

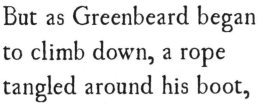

AHOY!

Ahhh...FINISHED AT LAAAAAST...!

headfirst over the side of his ship, stopping just before he hit the dock.

And standing upside down in front of him (or right side up, depending on which way you look at it) was the rat,

Snug Rumkin.

Snug Rumkin hauled Greenbeard back onto

The Golden Lettuce, where he landed with a SNAP!

"Oh no," said the rat gloomily, shaking his head.
"You've broken a leg. I'm not surprised."

(crunch, crunch)

"No, no,"
Greenbeard replied
cheerfully.
"It is only my
pirate sword."

He looked at his carrot fondly and took a bite.
"Ah! Still crisp, too!"

"That is not a sword!" growled Snug Rumkin.
"A *proper* pirate sword is sharp!"

THAT IS A CARROT!

Greenbeard stopped chewing. He got to his
feet, saying sternly, "Mr. Rumkin, I am
surprised at you. If the sword were sharp,
someone could get hurt!"

BUT THAT'S...

Snug Rumkin opened his mouth
to disagree, but Greenbeard
kept right on talking.

"Let us not be unpleasant, Mr. Rumkin."
He rummaged through his bag to find
another carrot. "I have need of a crew,
and I believe you will make an excellent
first mate."

YOUR CREW?? BUT...

"No, no, don't worry, my friend.
You will do fine."

ARRR...I'M NOT
WORRIED, BUT...

"Then it's settled!" said Greenbeard.

"Together we shall sail the seven seas,"
cried Greenbeard with a rousing cheer.

"We shall seek
treasure and have
lots and lots of...
adventure!"

"Treasure?" said Snug Rumkin.
"Lots and lots of treasure?"

Sob!

"Yes! Oh, yes!"
he cried as tears of
joy fell from his eyes.
At last, he was no
longer gloomy!

"Wait," said Greenbeard as a fine salt breeze began to blow. He took a deep, deep breath. "Ahhh... can you smell that?"

Snug Rumkin's whiskers twitched. "It smells like... like..."

"...like adventure!" said Greenbeard, and he laughed a hearty, piratey sort of laugh. "Weigh anchor!" he cried.

"Aye, aye, Captain," shouted Snug with a snappy salute.

As the stars twinkled in the night sky,
Greenbeard and Snug Rumkin sat on the deck of
The Golden Lettuce.

They were bound for adventure! Greenbeard was so
excited, so filled with joy, he burst into song!

"Arrrr!" said Snug. "What are you singing?
That is not a *proper* pirate song!"
But Greenbeard was singing too loudly to hear.

Snug cried, "No! NO! NOOOOOO!"

...with mold on my biscuits and grit in my claws,

I'm GREENBEARD the PIRATE,
It's adventure I seek,
'til my lettuce has wilted
or my boat springs a leak!

Yo, HO! Yo, HO! A pirate pig I beeeee...!

I think I shall start again...ahem...

Yo, HO! Yo, HO...!

NOOOooooOOO!

And so, as Snug Rumkin jammed his fingers in his ears and Greenbeard sang on (and on... and on...), The Golden Lettuce sailed for the horizon.

The many adventures of

GREENBEARD
The Pirate Pig

had begun.

Greenbeard the Pirate Pig

as sung by
Greenbeard

(lively, piratey tempo)

Yo, HO   Yo, HO! A pi-rate pig I be!   Yo, HO!

Yo, HO! I sail the se-ven seeas! With wind in my whis-kers

and salt in my pa-ws! With mold on my bis-cuits

and grit in my claws! I'm Greenbeard the Pi-rate, iiiii-iit's

adve-en-ture I seeek! 'Til my le- ttuce has wil-ted or...

my-y boat has sprung a leeeak!

The End

(THE BEGINNING)

COMING SOON!

On their next adventure,
Greenbeard and Snug discover
THE ISLE OF LOST and find
much more than treasure!

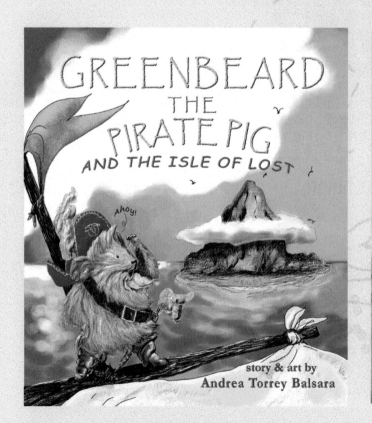

Greenbeard the Pirate Pig is back, and sailing the salty seas!
When he spies a lonely island, he and Snug Rumkin go exploring.
But they find much more than adventure... The rotten pirate, Kap'n Kale,
and his horrible first mate, Mr. Sweeny, have mousenapped
a shipload of orphans and are making them dig the island for treasure!

Wheeeee!

This way,
Wumkin!

No, no, Mr. Rumkin!
The treasure is this way!

Will the orphans be saved? Will Snug Rumkin ever find treasure of his own?
And will Greenbeard ever stop singing that song?

Andrea Torrey Balsara is a Canadian children's author and illustrator who writes and illustrates for ages 3 and up. She is involved with children's empowerment, and works to create stories that not only make children laugh, but makes them think. Her latest illustrated book, GREENBEARD THE PIRATE PIG, is a whimsical adventure about a guinea pig with a dream.

"Wonderful! What a delightful hero (and crew) ye have in Greenbeard! Oblivious to danger—focused on what CAN BE rather than the nay-saying of a well-intentioned rat...and the song is an added delight! We'd sail with Greenbeard any day!"

—Cap'n Slappy and ChumbuCket,
Founders of Talk Like a Pirate Day

CPSIA information can be obtained
at www.ICGtesting.com
Printed in the USA
LVOW06s0829140916
504557LV00004B/4/P